Copyright © 2020 DC Comics.
WONDER WOMAN and all related characters and
elements © and ™ DC Comics. WB SHIELD: ™ & ©
Warner Bros. Entertainment Inc.
(s20)

All rights reserved. Published in the United States by Random House Children's Books,
a division of Penguin Random House LLC, 1745 Broadway, New York, NY 10019, and in
Canada by Penguin Random House Canada Limited, Toronto. Random House and the colophon are registered trademarks
of Penguin Random House LLC.
rhcbooks.com
ISBN 978-0-593-30647-5 (hardcover) — ISBN 978-0-593-30648-2 (ebook)
Printed in the United States of America
10 9 8 7 6 5 4 3 2 1

Christmas Comes to Paradise Island!

By Lauren Clauss • Illustrated by Pernille Ørum

Wonder Woman created by William Moulton Marston

Random House New York

It was December 23, and Wonder Woman had just finished handing out Christmas presents at the animal shelter. She and the other volunteers had helped decorate it. Looking around, she wondered how she would be spending the holiday this year.

"I wish I could celebrate with my family," she said, sighing wistfully, "but we don't have Christmas on Paradise Island."

Then Wonder Woman had a wonderful idea—she could bring Christmas to her family!

She had always loved the holiday's shiny decorations and delicious sweets. Why *not* bring that joy to Paradise Island?

Wonder Woman rushed out to a store. She bought gifts, decorations, and food. Then she made a list of the best Christmas traditions she had experienced since leaving home. She was excited to share them with her family.

On the morning of Christmas Eve, Wonder Woman flew to Paradise Island. She was greeted by all her loved ones and friends, who were thrilled by her surprise visit.

"My sweet Diana," said Queen Hippolyta, greeting her daughter with a warm hug.

This is the perfect start to Christmas! Diana thought. *And it will only get better from here.*

After saying hello to everyone, Wonder Woman pulled out the list she had made.

"I'm here because I want to celebrate Christmas with you all!" she announced. "It's a holiday that is celebrated around the world, and I think it would be fun for us, too."

"Well," one Amazon asked, "how do we begin?"

"Let's start with something fun, like playing in the snow!" Diana suggested. "Children love to make snow people and have snowball fights around Christmastime."

"But it never snows here!" an Amazon reminded her.

"That's true," Diana replied. It really *had* been too long since she'd been home.

"I guess the gifts I brought you aren't very practical, then," Diana said, pulling sleds out of her bag.

"Wait," said another Amazon. "We don't need snow for these!" The Amazons raced down a hill on their sleds, enjoying the thrill.

Diana had an idea. "Let's eat!" she exclaimed. "I brought a traditional Christmas dessert for you. It's called fruitcake."

The Amazons dug in eagerly, but slowed down after tasting the so-called treat.

"That's okay," Diana said. "Many others don't like fruitcake much, either. . . . I think that's part of the tradition!"

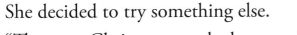

She decided to try something else.

"There are Christmas carols that people sing all season long!" she said. Diana tried to teach a group of Amazons one classic Christmas song, and a different group another song, so they could be carolers for each other. The Amazons learned quickly—and then launched into a caroling competition!

"This is not in the spirit of the season!" Diana said.

She thought for a moment.

"I know what we can do next," she said. "Let's decorate the island!"
She reached into her bag once more. "I brought material for making our
own decorations!"

Wonder Woman taught the Amazons how to string popcorn and cranberries into decorative garlands, and how to make pine cones and seashells into ornaments. She explained how people also use twinkling lights and inflatable characters to decorate their homes and yards.

But she hadn't brought any of those, since there was no electricity on Paradise Island.

Although the Amazons were enjoying themselves, Diana felt disappointed. Maybe the Amazons of Paradise Island just weren't meant to celebrate Christmas the way she knew it.

Then one of the Amazons picked up Diana's list and leafed through it. "What is this about a Christmas tree, Diana?" she asked.

Aha! Diana thought. There were plenty of trees on Paradise Island! But none of Diana's ornaments would stay on their leaves. Then someone climbed a tree and placed a star at the top. Unfortunately, it was too high up for anyone to see.

Diana hoped the most exciting part of her Christmas news would help the Amazons feel the joy of the holiday. She eagerly told them about Santa Claus.

"He is a jolly man who travels the world," she said, "bringing people together and leaving presents for children to open on Christmas morning! That's what the decorations are for—so he knows where to leave presents!"

"Oh, Diana," Queen Hippolyta said. "You are so very much like this . . . Santa Claus. You've brought us so much to share."

Everyone cheered.

"I'm glad you like the holiday," Diana said. "I realize some of these traditions must seem very strange to you."

Queen Hippolyta sat by her daughter. "Diana," she said gently, "decorations and presents and trees are nice, but what we are really celebrating is being with the people we love. And that is what you've brought us."

Working together, the Amazons made adjustments to Diana's Christmas traditions.

They made figures out of sand instead of snow,

decorated trees with objects from the island,

and made gifts for each other that they could use—

all while singing their own Christmas songs.

On Christmas morning, the Amazons exchanged
new armor and enjoyed the festive scenery.

Diana hugged her mother. Even though their Christmas celebration wasn't quite what she'd intended, she was thrilled that it was as spectacular as she had wanted it to be.

Diana loved being Wonder Woman, but she was enjoying being back with her fellow Amazons on Paradise Island. She knew it was important to spend time with her family and friends and remember where she came from. And she knew she'd be back next year!